W9-BUR-036

Charlie was a shepherd. He had
a cozy house, a big hat, a crook,
and a flock of fat sheep.

But everyone said,

"CHARLIE NEEDS A CLOAK"

story and pictures by

Tomie dePaola

Simon and Schuster Books for Young Readers
Published by Simon & Schuster Inc., New York

FOR DUCHIN & FLORENCE ♡♡

Copyright © 1973 by Thomas dePaola

All rights reserved
including the right of reproduction
in whole or in part in any form.

Published by Simon and Schuster Books for Young Readers
A Division of Simon & Schuster, Inc.
Simon & Schuster Building
Rockefeller Center
1230 Avenue of the Americas
New York, NY 10020

10

10 9 8 7   pbk

Simon and Schuster Books for Young Readers
is a trademark of Simon & Schuster, Inc.

Manufactured in the United States of America

Library of Congress Cataloging in Publication Data
DePaola, Thomas Anthony
    "Charlie needs a cloak."
    Summary: A shepherd shears his sheep, cards and
spins the wool, weaves and dyes the cloth, and sews
a beautiful new red cloak.
    1. Woolen and worsted manufacture—Juvenile literature
2. Tailoring—Juvenile literature. [1. Wool. 2. Clothing
and dress]   I. Title
TS1626.D4   646.4′5   73-16365
ISBN 0-671-66466-2
ISBN 0-671-66467-0 pbk

Poor Charlie!

He really needed a new cloak.

So, in the spring, Charlie sheared
his sheep.

He washed the wool,

and carded the wool to straighten
it out.

Then Charlie spun the wool into yarn.

Charlie wanted a red cloak, so he picked some pokeweed berries during the late summer, and boiled them over a fire.

Then Charlie dyed the yarn red in the berry juice.

After the yarn was dry, Charlie put the strands on the loom.

And every fall evening, he wove
the yarn into cloth.

Charlie put the cloth on the table
and cut it into pieces.

He pinned the pieces together,

and sewed them.

And then, when winter came,

Charlie had a beautiful new red cloak.

shear-To clip the wool from a sheep.

card-To untangle wool with a comb or brush.

spin-To twist wool into yarn.

weave-To twist thread into cloth.

sew-To fasten together with thread.

cloak-A coat without sleeves.